Rebellion

Fisk rebels against the worst organist ever encountered in more than four decades of filling his church with heavenly music. But when the rector blames him for the resulting dissonance, must he make the ultimate sacrifice?

Evolution

Syndi believes her father hates her because of the third arm that her parents constantly fight about. But, then she grabs an opportunity to prove its special advantages to the world.

As a reporter, editor, business writer, and marketing communications consultant, F.I. Goldhaber produced news stories, feature articles, essays, editorial columns, and reviews for newspapers, corporations, governments, and non-profits in five states. Now, her poems, short stories, novelettes, essays, and reviews appear in paper, electronic, and audio magazines, ezines, newspapers, calendars, and anthologies. She published five erotica novels and a novella under another name.

In addition to paper, electronic, and audio publications, F.I. shares her words at events in Portland, Seattle, Salem, Keizer and on the radio. She appeared at venues such as Wordstock, Oregon Literary Review, PDX SynesthiA, bookstores, libraries, and community colleges; gives presentations on subjects as diverse as marketing, writing erotica, and building volunteer organizations; and taught Introduction to Indie Publishing at Portland Community College and as a weekend intensive.

http://goldhaber.net/

Table of Contents

Acknowledgements

Many thanks to all those I have learned from through the years, especially the Wordos professional writers workshop and Larry Brooks. Thanks also to those who have freely shared their knowledge online, notably Dean Wesley Smith and Kristine Kathryn Rusch. Those who inspired me to pursue writing from an early age include Ruth Wright, my fifth and sixth grade teacher at Randolph Elementary School in Huntsville, Alabama; Nancy Travis, my freshman English teacher at Clear Creek High School in Texas; and most prominently my parents, Jerry and Bev Goldhaber. Very special thanks to my editor, Laurie Lawhon of Fine Tune Your Words, and my beloved husband Joel Goldhaber.

Rebellion

Compromise his music
or sacrifice his soul?

F.I. Goldhaber

𝕽ebellion

By F.I. Goldhaber

During Fisk's forty-six years at Christ Episcopal Church in East Bay Harbor, Connecticut, organists came and went. While most played for several years, a few stayed only months. Fisk remembered them all by their hands. Matthew had short, pudgy fingers, yet he manipulated Fisk's keys with a firm touch and coaxed out wondrous harmonies. Lenora fondled Fisk's keys with thin, expressive fingers requiring him to stay alert lest he miss a note. Roger's hands, like soft clouds, caressed Fisk's keys towards new heights in sound.

Other than his well-worn bench — the varnish polished away by organists' vestments to reveal the intricate grain of fine oak — Fisk showed remarkably few signs of age. Two of his stops, stuck in the Off position, resisted all attempts to use them. A few of his keys had chips or gouges. But Fisk still impressed worshipers with his music. Although he didn't agree with every organist's style and some didn't value his abilities, Fisk had always respected their individual gifts. He concentrated on delivering the highest quality performance, within their limitations and his, that honored the artistry of his creators.

But, Ms. Dagger Nails demolished his opinion that every organist had something worthy to offer. She had appeared as a last-minute substitute and Fisk only expected her to play for one or two services until the Rector found a permanent organist. Instead, the tiny woman had abused his keys and ignored his pedals for the past dozen Sundays. Fisk didn't think he could abide her ineptitude any longer, but he despaired of the church ever removing her.

Some musicians trod on Fisk's pedal keyboard with the heavy feet of clog dancers; others two-stepped agilely, skipping among the long wooden keys. But, Ms. Dagger Nails played with her heels perched on the rail of his bench where competent organists merely rested their feet for a moment between hymns. Without the weight of the bass tones from the pedal pipes, Ms. Dagger Nails' attempts at making music screamed annoyingly throughout the church. She found no use for Fisk's third manual; she missed at least one note for every five she hit; and she chose atrocious registrations, selecting the least pleasant sounds from the hundreds of timbres offered by Fisk's palette.

When his power switch flipped on to wake him two weeks before Palm Sunday, Fisk soon realized he must endure Ms. Dagger Nails' torture through yet another service. *I've been filling this church with inspired music every week for decades. I deserve more respect*! He pondered his predicament while Ms. Dagger Nails fiddled with her sheets of music. *I can no longer accept mistreatment without protest. I am a work of art and I should sound like one.* He resolved to rid himself of his tormentor by Easter, his favorite service.

At that moment, Ms. Dagger Nails pressed a key in her tentative manner as if requesting permission to torment Fisk's manuals. He refused to open the pipe fully, choking off the airflow. The expected musical note became a distorted squeak that reflected off the wooden rafters of the vast sanctuary and echoed eerily between the lofty granite walls.

Ms. Dagger Nails gasped, but she pressed again. Fisk resisted her touch, stopping the key halfway down to truncate the note. Despite the cacophony, Ms. Dagger Nails continued. Although Fisk grudgingly admired her fortitude, he maintained his rebellion throughout her entire prelude. J.S. Bach sounded as arrhythmic and atonal as Edgar Varèse.

Let the Rector ignore her atrocious playing now! Fisk added an extra discordant note just for good measure.

He could hear murmurs from the congregants who shifted on the dozens of stark wooden pews below him. The choir, standing in three rows on either side of his console, sang louder than usual, trying to drown out the awful noise. Lately, since they had noone to work with them, only half of them sang in true key. When Fisk helped them harmonize, they didn't sound too bad. But, today, the rustle of their worn, blue polyester robes produced better harmony. Rector Bob ended the service early, before Ms. Dagger Nails could mangle the Recessional hymn.

The following Sunday, Ms. Dagger Nails returned. Fisk groaned in frustration when he sensed her diminutive presence on his bench. He refused to respond when the lacquered points of her fingernails scraped at the imitation ivory of his keys. She jabbed harder, pinching the key between her nail and the action, forcing Fisk to relent because he could not tolerate the pain. But he stopped the airflow to his pneumatic motors and every note screeched dissonantly. Fisk cringed, ashamed that his beautiful pipes could produce such ululations.

A few days later, a technician subjected Fisk to a rigorous physical exam. The man removed and replaced several of Fisk's two thousand, four hundred forty-four pipes. He adjusted all fifty-six of Fisk's stops — fixing the two that were jammed in the Off position, much to Fisk's relief. The technician inspected a number of the thin, aluminum rods connecting keys to pipe valves. He tested every Swell manual shutter control and depressed each of the one hundred seventy-eight keys on Fisk's three manuals as well as all thirty-two pedals.

Fisk enjoyed the gentle reverence of the man's inspection. The technician obviously valued a quality instrument, and Fisk appreciated the fine tuning. He made sure that every note spoke with the proper tone, filling the old stone church with a divinely mystical sound. The inspection complete, he overheard the technician explaining to the Rector that Fisk was in good condition for an organ his age.

"I didn't find anything that could cause Carole the problems you mentioned. Still, all the salt in the air here isn't good for any instrument. You probably need to consider refurbishing or replacing this organ in the near future. If organists are having trouble with it now, you may want to do that sooner, rather than later."

Fisk knew the church did not have funds to spare for a refurbishing. He wondered where the Rector found the money to pay the technician. The past few years, pleas for funds from the pulpit had grown increasingly impassioned. Never before had he heard a Rector constantly badger parishioners for support. Until recently, a need mentioned one Sunday resulted in accolades by the next for the donor who had stepped forward to meet it.

"Do you think it could be the fault of the musician rather than the instrument?" the Rector asked. "Carole's a pianist, she hasn't had much experience playing organ."

Fisk suppressed the urge to allow a smug chord to escape through his pipes.

"I appreciate good church music as much as anyone, and I know there's a vast range in abilities from one player to the next," the technician said. "But you can't blame sticky keys and squeaky pipes on the organist."

Fisk's bellows sagged.

Rector Bob sighed. "What kind of money are we talking about?"

"A proper refurbishment's gonna run you fifty to sixty thousand."

Fisk heard the Rector whistle. "That much?"

The technician cleared his throat. "Yeah. Takes expensive materials — leather and exotic woods — and some're hard to find. I'll need several weeks, if not months. Once you replace all the leather, you have to go in and adjust the tension on thousands of hinges connecting the valve mechanisms to the keyboards."

The technician scratched his beard. "You know, you could buy a used electronic organ for maybe fifteen to twenty thousand. Not going to give you the same quality of sound as this beauty," he patted Fisk's oak cabinet, "but you could take out this console and fit an electronic organ in its place and leave those gorgeous pipes in for looks."

Fisk's burnished zinc display pipes soared from above his console toward the ceiling. They embraced the round frame of the large rose window over the church's main entrance. The tall, narrow arches of the lancet stained-glass panels were flanked by additional pipes on either side. All together he made an impressive display that he always tried to honor with his music.

"I'll bet," the technician continued, "most people won't know the difference."

Fisk closed every pallet to prevent a moan from escaping. He had never considered the possibility that his rebellion could cost him his position at the church.

"Well, I disagree with you on that note." Rector Bob tapped out a C major scale. Although he had never tried to play Fisk, the pastor could coax a simple hymn out of the grand piano in the chapel. "I think my parishioners appreciate the beauty of this old guy's tone. Music is still one of the best ways for a church to attract and keep members."

Fisk *had* noticed fewer people attending each additional week that the interim organist played. He had expected the Rector to take action sooner, if only to stop the exodus.

"Still, if we keep having problems..."

Fisk held his wind.

"We certainly don't have the funds for a restoration. I can't imagine trying to raise that much money — not right now with attendance down and the economy costing so many of our parishioners their jobs and homes." Rector Bob sighed again. "I suppose we would have to consider an electronic replacement. Do the more expensive ones sound anything like a real pipe organ?"

The technician laughed. "Well, I guess that depends on who's listening. Look, Reverend, this instrument set the church back what, a quarter mil? You're not going to get anything like it for ten or twenty grand. But you'll get something that won't need as much maintenance. With a nice set of speakers, a decent organist can give you an acceptable musical program. Given the acoustics you have in here, I'll bet any instrument'll sound pretty good." The technician snapped his fingers and the two men stood next to Fisk, listening to the sound reverberate through the stately old church.

"What would we do with this console?" The rector's voice cracked a little. Fisk had been installed almost a quarter of a century before Rector Bob joined the church. In his first sermon, the pastor had said that his love of good music had influenced his decision to accept the appointment.

"You could stash it somewhere in case things turn around and you can raise restoration money. Best bet, though, is sell it for parts — not that you'll get much unless you throw in the pipes. Then you have to pay for reconstruction. Doubt if you'd get enough for the whole organ to cover that."

The rest of the conversation did not register

with Fisk, their words blurred by the torment of his choice: accept Ms. Dagger Nails' abuse and allow her to play without interference or get replaced, gutted for parts, and dumped on a trash heap somewhere.

The artisans who had created him had designed him for a life that, with proper care, could span centuries. How could the Rector consider destroying Fisk after less than half of one?

The technician forgot to turn off his power, leaving Fisk alone with his memories. His music had accompanied four thousand, seven hundred ninety-six Sunday morning Eucharists, two thousand, three hundred ninety-eight Thursday evening choir rehearsals, eight hundred fifty-two weddings, seven hundred twenty-seven funerals, and one hundred ninety-two recitals. He thought of the many brides who had gushed about how they had always dreamed of a wedding in Christ Church with Fisk's sublime accompaniment for their walk down the aisle. He remembered somber widows discussing their husbands' favorite hymns and how only Fisk could play them right. And how many people had joined the church after attending a recital or concert and recognizing what Fisk could add to their spiritual experience?

Fisk allowed himself a snort from his windchest. *No*! He would not compromise, even if the church did not replace Ms. Dagger Nails with a real organist. Better to die an ignoble death than have anyone regard him as a second-rate instrument. Let the church try to replace him with one of those electronic fandangles. How could anyone even call such a contrivance an organ? Some of the congregants would protest, even if they could not raise the money to save him. At least they would remember him for the artistry of music he had produced for decades rather than the few months of horrible sounds Ms. Dagger Nails forced out of him.

Fisk let out his wind and strengthened his resolve. He knew the church had served East Bay Harbor for more than a hundred years. At one time, it had attracted many of the community's movers and shakers. The parishioners had worked long and hard to raise the money required to purchase and install him in 1965. They had even built the gallery in the back of the sanctuary just to accommodate him and his pipes. Fisk would not lower Christ Church's musical standards or his own!

On Palm Sunday, Ms. Dagger Nails returned, but Fisk had devised a new plan. When she pressed a key, he sent air through the wrong pipe. For every note she tried to play, Fisk chose something different. Middle C became B, two octaves higher. When she selected a flute sound, Fisk supplied trumpet instead.

Flustered, Ms. Dagger Nails knocked a page of music to the floor. When she bent down to pick it up, Fisk let out a low E-flat on the bassoon stop. The organist pushed herself off his bench and ran from the choir loft in tears. She had not even finished her prelude. The choir sang a capella for the rest of the service — dreadfully off key. The deacons gathered the Offertory in silence, except for the tap, tap, tap of envelopes dropping onto collection plates. During Communion, footsteps echoed forlornly throughout the church while everyone walked down the candlelit center aisle to the granite altar. No one sang; no one played, and Fisk awaited his inevitable fate, his expression pedal drooping.

Once again, Fisk found himself alone. No one turned off his power after Ms. Dagger Nails' abrupt exit. Hours passed before Rector Bob ventured into the choir loft above the sanctuary. He brought a tape measure and several sheets of paper with him. Fisk sat silent while the pastor pulled the tape across his console's width, depth, and height, and scribbled numbers down on the sheets of paper. Fisk cringed when he heard the Rector muttering about fit, costs, and sound.

The Rector's hand rested on the power switch and Fisk prepared to go to sleep, perhaps forever. Without warning, Rector Bob's fingers dropped to one of Fisk's manuals and he again tapped out a C major scale. He muttered words Fisk could not make out.

He loves my music; I have to make him understand. Fisk opened his pipes in sequence to play a verse of "Amazing Grace." He didn't move his keys, but he put his heart and soul into each note, making sure they all rang true.

Fisk had not thought about how the Rector would react to an organ generating its own music. Rector Bob dropped onto Fisk's bench with a thud and his feet pressed several pedals at once. Surprised by the sudden weight on the bass keys, Fisk could not stop the notes and the discordant combination brayed through the church. Before Fisk could recover, Rector Bob pressed the power switch.

Power coursed through Fisk's circuits awakening him once more, to his great surprise and delight.

Colored light from the stained-glass windows danced across the silver verticals of his pipes. Fisk sensed the unfamiliar weight of someone new on his bench. He let a little air hiss in his windchest, just to show he knew someone expected him to make music, and raised his bellows in anticipation. Long elegant fingers, with nails appropriately trimmed short and filed smooth, ran an arpeggio across his Great manual. Feet encased in proper organ shoes stroked the pedal keyboard. With new hope, Fisk let the notes ring out fully in response, reveling in a firm but gentle touch.

Rector Bob stepped into the choir loft. "I really appreciate your agreeing to play for Easter services on such short notice, Stephanie. We haven't been able to fill the organist's position and our interim volunteer isn't able to make it. Please take all the time you need to practice. Also, the choir hoped you'd consider working with them a bit during their rehearsal tomorrow evening."

"I've always wanted an opportunity to play a Fisk organ." Stephanie spoke in melodious tones and Fisk wanted to hear her sing. "I didn't know the position here was vacant until the secretary called me about playing for Easter."

Fisk waited for Rector Bob to warn the newcomer about his problems, but the priest left the loft without saying anything else.

Stephanie reset several of Fisk's combination pistons in sensible registrations, then played "Bach's Toccata and Fugue in D Minor." Her weight shifted easily on the bench with the movement of her hands across all three manuals, while her feet danced on the pedals. Fisk delighted in the touch of an organist who could play, who knew how to coax the proper tone from his pipes. After the hell of the last several months, Fisk had found heaven at last.

For the first time in weeks, Fisk looked forward to Easter Sunday. Maybe if he performed his very best, Stephanie would consider staying on. Fisk gave Stephanie everything he had, responding to the organist's light touch with smooth action and true, clear notes. Their music filled the church and pride filled Fisk's heart again.

When the last notes drifted away, Rector Bob stepped back into the loft. "You certainly know how to bring out the best in the old boy." He patted Fisk's console. "Why don't you stop by the parsonage when you're done here, Stephanie, and we can talk about the organist's position."

"Absolutely," the organist responded.

Fisk wanted to sing and make his pipes dance, but he feared startling the Rector again. Instead he waited eagerly for Stephanie's next piece.

ℜ

Evolution

Three arms: transformational
advantage or freak mutation?

F.I. Goldhaber

Evolution

F.I. Goldhaber

Syndi tossed her carrysack into the closet by the front door and trudged down the narrow hallway to her room. She slammed the door, threw herself on the bed, and buried her face in her pillow.

"Stop getting upset, it's just the same thing as always," she blurted out through her tears. *Same thing or not, still hurts.* She wiped one sleeve across her eyes. *Crying doesn't change anything.* Rolling off, she used two hands to flip the bed up into the wall while she powered up her 'puter with her third.

The holiday meant no school tomorrow, so she could delay doing her homework without getting in trouble. She logged onto *World of SymMaul.* There, no one called her deformed, or a mutant, or a freak. No one online cared if she was only ten. No one in *SymMaul* dared torment the only person who had retrieved five golden keys and advanced to the third level after just two weeks in the game, all without twinking.

Syndi's sym spun around and activated her flame thrower, killing the orc stalking her and grabbing the bronze mace it had aimed at her head.

"Syndi."

She kept her eyes tuned to the screen. Another orc peered out from behind a boulder in front of the cave opening.

"Syndi!" This time her mother's voice had a do-not-ignore urgency.

Syndi paused the game and logged off. *I'd better remember to take care of that orc the minute I sign back on or it'll gank me 'fore I get a chance to react.*

"Yes, Mom." Syndi skipped into the common area to find her mother stirring something that smelled edible in a pot on the stove.

"I need you to assemble the Solstice tree before your dad gets here in ..." Mom checked her Link, "less than an hour."

Syndi rolled her eyes. *Maybe he'll have to work late.* Mom and Dad together in the same room meant more hostilities than SymMaul without as much fun. After all, Syndi couldn't take her parents out with a flamethrower when they insisted on getting together for holiday dinners.

She retrieved the box from under Mom's bed, dumped the pieces out onto the table, and put them together until they looked like the picture. When she heard the ringtones from the intercom, Syndi whispered under her breath, "Bet they start arguing before we sit down." She opened the door and took the boxes from her dad.

"How's my girl?" He rumpled her hair and she rolled her eyes again.

"Fine, Dad." *Like you wouldn't give anything to have someone else as your girl.* She stuck the boxes with the others Mom was arranging around the tree.

"Good evening, Evelyn." Dad handed a bottle to Mom. "I brought some of that pomcran juice you two like so much."

"Thanks, Robert." She returned to the stove and stirred the pot's contents again. "Dinner needs to simmer a little longer. Shall we open presents first?" She smoothed the bottom of her pink sweater over the waistband of her black slacks.

Mom always looked so slender and tidy, especially when Dad showed up, as usual, all rumpled. His belly protruded over his belt, his shirt had several stains on it and had pulled half out of his pants. Syndi sighed and followed her parents back to the tree.

Her mom handed her a green and red box. "Here, Syndi, you open the one from your dad first."

Probably another lame shirt. He always wanted her to wear loose fitting tops with two sleeves and hide her third arm underneath. Her mom had taught her how to take apart extra-large men's shirts and use the additional fabric to make tops with three sleeves. Lately, when she had to stay with her dad, Syndi just dressed the way he wanted, but stuffed one of her homemade shirts in her carrysack, and changed at school. She only got in trouble when she forgot to change back before she came home.

Syndi used her thumbnail to loosen the Velcro that kept the reusable plastic wrapping in place. Inside she found new underwear and this time Dad hadn't gotten the childish kind with 'toon characters on them. "Thanks, Dad. These are bruce."

"I take it that's a good thing?" He looked confused. Mom must've bought the undies.

"Yeah, Dad, these are what grown-up girls wear."

Mom handed a blue package to Dad. He folded back the wrapping, lifted the book from inside, held it up to his nose, and took a deep breath. "Ahh, lovely. Thank you, Evelyn. It's so wonderful to see real books printed on actual paper. Don't know how you always manage to find them, but I certainly do enjoy them."

Syndi refrained from telling her father that Mom had purchased several dozen online for almost nothing one year and kept them under her bed to dole out at holidays. Dad already had shelves and shelves of books at his place, but he seemed to treasure each one that she and Mom gave him. Why he wanted the musty old things, Syndi never could figure.

Dad gave Mom the usual pair of tickets to see the next *SymPun* concert. "Oh, thanks, Robert. I really want to see this program." She'd probably sell them online. She usually did.

"Here, Syndi." Mom handed her a package wrapped in yellow, her favorite color. "See what you think of this."

Syndi opened the wrapping to find a skirt made from the bruceiest shimmery fabric she had ever seen and a black, three-armed top with a metallic heart on it. It looked like the right size and didn't have crooked seams in odd places. "Bruce leesiest, Mom." She dropped them and wrapped all three arms around her. "That is the leesiest of the bruces."

Her mom squeezed her back. "Why don't you go try it on and make sure they fit?"

Syndi rushed back to her room, stripped off her flannel shirt and tossed it at the closet. She slid into the shimmery fabric, pulled the top over her head, and pushed her arms into the sleeves. She turned in front of the mirror on the door admiring how well the shirt fit her body, including the extra arm that extended from her right side. The fabric clung to the protruding rib bone that supported the arm, but the heart prevented it from looking odd.

When she charged out of her room, angry

words brought her to a halt before she rounded the corner.

"I suppose you don't care that the World Government Council has added this to the In-Uteri Deformities Act, which means Syndi will always be the only three-armed kid in the world?" Syndi could practically hear Dad spitting.

"I know you think she's some kind of freak. But, she's an intelligent, precocious little girl who *you* don't appreciate. I promised I would never slice up my child like this." Syndi didn't have to see to know that her mother lifted her pink top and pointed to the jagged scar on her right side.

"And what if Syndi's condition had required you to have in-uterine surgery? What would you have done?"

Syndi leaned against the wall and slid to the floor. The argument had never gone this direction before. She waited to hear Mom's answer.

"You idiot. The only reason I got involved with you in the first place is because I suspected we had complimentary genes. That's why I wouldn't sign the Civil Union papers until after the DNA testing showed we could have children without genetic manipulation or risk of deformity."

"You're a gene zealot?" Dad sounded shocked.

"Not exactly. I mean, I don't like the idea of gene manipulation. But, mostly I didn't want my baby to spend the first two years of her life, like I did, in and out of the hospital because of problems caused by in-uterine surgery."

"I know that, Evelyn, and I know your mother never fully recovered from the operation. But, in-uterine surgery has come such a very long way since you were born. Still, you chose to ruin Syndi's life. Look at all the trouble she has in school. And she has no friends."

"How can you say she has trouble in school when she's advanced two grade levels? She's two years younger than most of the kids in her class. Did you ever consider that that might keep her from making friends?"

Syndi sighed. They had returned to familiar topics. She may as well join them.

"I'm not talking about her grades, Evelyn. You know that."

"Well, she has lots of online friends."

"Evelyn."

"I gave up everything for her. I got involved with you instead of someone else, someone I might have wanted to stay with for longer than it took to get permission to have a baby. Now, I can't even get a date 'cause men who like kids want someone they can have their own with."

Syndi heard a loud gasp — she wasn't sure if it came from her father or her mother — followed by stomping feet and a slamming door.

She didn't know quite how to react. On the one hand, Dad leaving early meant she probably wouldn't get a tummy ache eating dinner. On the other hand, she already felt queasy given Mom's confession. But, on the other hand, if this kept Dad away or even meant she didn't have to go over to his place all the time... She smiled, pushed herself back up the wall, and turned the corner to find her mom sitting with her head resting in her hands.

"The shirt fits like skin and I love the skirt, Mom. They're really, really breezy."

Mom lifted her head and gave Syndi half a smile. "Hope you don't mind eating Solstice stew for the next few days. Without your dad, we're going to have lots of leftovers."

Syndi slammed her carrysack into the closet, stomped to her room, and threw the door closed with all the force she could muster. She looked in the mirror and sniveled. Her new shirt had a big hole in the middle and the heart was torn half off. Even if she stitched it back on, the shirt could never be the perfect shirt she had worn to school for the first time that morning.

"Dad's right, I am a freak," she told the mirror. Syndi peeled off the shirt, wadded it into a ball, and stuffed it in the back of her closet. She pulled on one of the shapeless shirts her dad preferred that she wear and sat down at the screen to do her homework. But, as soon as she finished the reading assignment and switched over to her math module, she stuck her third arm out through the shirt buttons so she could manipulate the number pad without taking her fingers off the letters. When she completed her spelling, she went to check in with her mom.

"I finished my homework..." Syndi stopped short when she realized her mom was talking on her Link.

"I've avoided press interviews for ten years now, Jask. Why in the world should I make an exception for you?" Her mom pursed her lips while whoever she was talking to replied. "I'm sorry, no. I want Syndi to have a normal childhood."

"Awww, Mom. Please." Syndi tugged on her mom's arm. "What's normal about me?"

"Hang on." Mom turned and held her finger against the mute button on her earpiece. "What do you mean?"

"I mean, why do you always rant about me having a normal childhood? If you wanted everything normal for me whydn't you cut this off in the first place?" Syndi held up the extra arm and wondered how much it would cost to get it cut off now.

Her mom closed her eyes and sighed. "Do you want to talk to a reporter, Syndi? He would post what you told him on the Net where all your friends could see it."

"Don't have any friends, not real ones anyway. But maybe a story on the Net would get me some." Syndi grinned. *Or at least pwn the twinks who ripped my shirt.* She shrugged. "And why would I tell him anything I didn't want friends to read?"

Releasing the mute button, Mom said, "Apparently, my daughter is willing to talk to you. However, you cannot meet with her unless I am present, you cannot use any video during the interview, and I reserve the right to terminate if I don't like the type of questions you ask."

After Mom entered all the details about their meeting with the reporter into her Link, she turned to Syndi. "If you really want to do this, I'll go along. But don't tell your father."

"If it's on the Net, he's gonna find out." *And maybe he'll disown me.* She grinned.

"Yes, but if he learns about it beforehand he will try to stop you."

Syndi rolled her eyes. "Pods, Mom. Give me some cred. Don't ya think I know that? Dad's the last one I'd tell." *About anything.*

"Actually, you probably should let him know before the story appears. He might not get quite as upset if he learns about it from you rather than stumbling over it himself."

"I guess." *Like I could do anything that didn't upset him.*

The night before her interview, Syndi dug her torn shirt out of the back of the closet and smoothed away the wrinkles. She stitched the heart back in place, sewed a glittery 3 over the hole, and added a couple more to the back. In the morning, she asked her mom to tie her straight blondish hair into three tails instead of two.

They rode the underground to the Media Centre and Syndi had a difficult time sitting still on the hard seat. The excitement made her feet twitch and her rear end wriggle. Even the stares and mutterings from other passengers didn't bother her today. The train stopped underneath the Media Centre so they didn't have to go outside in the frigid cold. They climbed up the wide, stone stairs to the huge lobby filled with all kinds of artificial plants and stills from vid shows. Syndi squirmed while Mom showed their identity papers to get passes so they could ride up the lift.

When the doors slid open on the thirtieth floor, a blonde woman younger than Mom led them into a tiny room just big enough to hold a table and three chairs. Shortly after the blonde left, a tall, skinny guy with dark skin, red hair, and a braided beard came in.

"Evelyn." He nodded at Mom. "Syndi, I'm Jask. So glad you could talk to me today." He waved his hand around. "Sorry about the size of the room, but this is the only one without video equipment." He pointed to buttons in the center of the table. "I'll make an audio of our conversation, though, if that's acceptable."

Her mom nodded and Syndi grinned.

Jask sat down. Syndi took the chair across from him and put two hands in her lap and one on the table.

Jask flipped one of the switches. "Tell me, Syndi, when did you first realize you weren't the same as the other children?"

Syndi scrunched up her face. "Dunno. Always knew I was different. Mom told me I was special. Dad kept trying to hide this." She lifted her lower right hand from her lap and wiggled her fingers.

"Do you wish you only had two arms like everyone else?"

"Nomdom, no. Why'd I want that? Everything's easier with three hands: schoolwork, chores," Syndi jumped up, wrapped two arms around her mom's waist, and laced her fingers with Mom's using her free hand, "even hugs." If she told the world all the bruce things about three arms, maybe some of the kids at school would stop tormenting her.

Jask waited until she sat down before asking another question. "Why is schoolwork easier?"

Syndi giggled. "'Cause I can type with two hands and move the pointer or use the number pad with my third."

"Is that why you do so well on the games?"

"Well, it helps a little. But mostly, I do so well 'cause I pay attention and understand how the games work."

"Do the children at school give you a hard time?"

Syndi bit her lip for a moment to keep from bursting into tears, then lifted her chin. "They're just jealous 'cause I can beat kids way older than me in any game. I get better grades and I always finish my craft assignments before they do." Of course, none of this added to her popularity, but Jask, and the Net, didn't need to know that.

Jask looked up at her mom. "Has Syndi ever had a scan to see if she uses her brain differently than other kids her age?"

"No. Except for her arm, she's a normal, happy, healthy, ten-year-old. I've seen no reason to subject her to unnecessary medical procedures."

"Have you ever considered that using a third arm may have triggered an increase in mental capacity?"

"Doesn't really matter, does it?" Her mom, who stood behind Syndi with one hand on her right shoulder, tightened her grip.

Jask raised one eyebrow. "It might. Doctors perform thousands of in-uterine surgeries every year. In poorer countries, arms are amputated after babies are born. What if these children would have better lives with their third arm?"

"I didn't refuse to have surgery so Syndi could function as some kind of lab rat. I just didn't like the idea of cutting my baby apart before she was even born."

"I understand that." Jask smiled. Syndi liked his smile, all dimply with dark skin setting off his white teeth. "But, the truth is, Syndi's different. If we found out why ... Do you know how many times the WGC has rejected legislation rescinding the In-Uteri Deformities Act? If we can provide evidence that this is an evolutionary improvement and not a disfiguring anomaly, we could possibly get the WGC to stop requiring woman who refuse in-uterine surgery to have abortions."

Her mom released Syndi's shoulders and sat down in the other chair with a thud. "Why are you doing this?"

The man opened his shirt and showed the white scar under his right arm. "I was born in Congolabon. The doctors cut off my arm two days later." He re-buttoned his shirt.

"But that doesn't explain ..."

"I cover InterNic so I read the weekly reports. I saw the notice that a ten-year-old had gotten approval to enter the teen gaming area and then watched her take over World of SymMaul. The name jostled a memory and I found a piece in the archives about the reprimand you received for refusing surgery, abortion, and amputation." He shrugged. "I did some more research, found Syndi's school records and the dissolution of your CU with her father. I started to wonder what was causation and what was just correlation. I've already gotten approval for MediaCor to pay for the scan. I assure you it's completely non-invasive and safe."

Mom put her elbows on the table and leaned her head in her hands.

Syndi didn't understand all of what Jask said, but figured getting something changed at the WGC would impress her schoolmates. "It's okay, Mom. I don't care if they scan my brain." Syndi patted her mom's shoulder. "I mean, I like my third arm a lot, and I'm glad you didn't let 'em cut it off. But it's really hard being the only kid in school with one. I wouldn't mind some company." *Or at least someone telling the world I'm not a freak.*

Her mom lifted her head and looked at Syndi, tears glistening in her eyes. "You don't wish I'd had the surgery?"

Syndi shook her head hard enough to make her tails swat at her face. "Nope. I'd rather have three arms than all the friends in school." A lie, but it would make Mom feel better. Syndi hated to see her cry.

"You want to let them scan your brain?"

"Why not?" Syndi shrugged.

Mom looked at Jask. "I want MediaCor to agree to pay all expenses and keep our identity and where we live out of the reports."

"No problem. Now, may I ask Syndi some more questions?"

"Look, Dad." Syndi reached around her father to flip through the pictures on the screen. "My brain's way leesisier than all those other kids." Jask had sent a preview of the story that would appear on the Net tomorrow. It included scans comparing her brain with half a dozen other ten-year-olds. All the other scans looked alike. Hers had way more colored splotches.

"What has your mother done, now?" He thumped his fist on the table so hard the dishes rattled.

"Mom didn't do anything." Syndi stood up and put all three fists on her hips. She had hoped Dad would be proud of her for once. "I talked to the reporter, I wanted to tell my story. Look." She pointed to the pertinent paragraph, the one she had read to herself a dozen times before showing the story to her dad. "He says my third arm is an improvement. That I my brain more efficiently 'cause of it." Would Jask's words impress the kids at school? They certainly didn't seem to mean much to her father.

Dad leaned his forehead against his palms and his elbows against the table. "Well, at least he didn't include any identification. If I don't say anything, hopefully none of my colleagues will make the connection."

"Come on, Dad, log on." Syndi flipped off the screen. "'Course they'll know — how many ten year olds have three arms?"

"Most of my colleagues don't even know I have a daughter and even with those who know that much, I certainly haven't shared your," he cleared his throat, "uniqueness."

Syndi shouldn't have expected the article to make a difference. "You know, I don't have to come over here every week."

His head snapped up. "Oh, Syndi." He wrapped his arms around her and pulled her into his lap. "I'm sorry. Look, if it had been up to me, your mother would have had the surgery. I didn't, and don't, think it's fair to saddle you with the burdens you've faced being different from everyone else." He gave Syndi a squeeze. "Now, I get your mother telling me she only ever saw me as a sperm donor. Not that I didn't always wonder what a woman as beautiful as Evelyn ever wanted with a nerd like me." He put one hand under her chin. "At least you got her good looks."

He smiled, but she could see tears in his eyes. "You need to understand that the one thing I've never regretted, the one thing I feel incredibly lucky about, is that I get to be your dad. That makes the rest of it all worthwhile."

Syndi stared at him. "You want to be my dad?"

"Of course I do, baby."

"But, you always want me to hide my arm. You're always yelling at Mom for not cutting it off. You hide me from your friends." Syndi's lower lip twitched.

"I hide you from my colleagues, not my friends. I work in genetic research and manipulation. If my boss knew ..." He put one hand on each of her cheeks. "Despite what your mother says, I don't think you're a freak. I just hate seeing what the other kids do to you. I never had very many friends when I was young, but I still had it way better than you do. Even though you try to hide it, I know how unhappy their harassment makes you." He released her face.

Syndi scrunched up her nose. "'S that why you always want me to wear two-armed shirts?"

He nodded. "I know that's what people see first, I know that's why you get tormented all the time in school. But you are not your arm. I want people to get a chance to understand that Syndi is not a three-armed freak."

She rested her head against his shoulder. "You can be bruce, Dad, sometimes. 'Specially when you and Mom aren't fighting about me."

He chuckled. "Maybe instead of changing how often you come here, I should just reduce how often your mother and I get together."

Syndi smiled. Whether or not Jask's article got her some respect at school, it had already helped her understand Dad so much better.